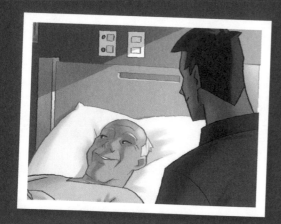

Family Is a Superpower is published by
Capstone Editions
a Capstone imprint
1710 Roe Crest Drive
North Mankato, Minnesota 56003
www.mycapstone.com

STAR41362

Superman created by Jerry Siegel and Joe Shuster
by special arrangement with the Jerry Siegel family

Cataloging-in-Publication Data is available on the
Library of Congress website.

ISBN: 978-1-68446-035-9 (hardcover)
ISBN: 978-1-68446-040-3 (eBook)

Book design by Bob Lentz

Printed in the United States of America.
PA49

words by **MICHAEL DAHL**

pictures by **OMAR LOZANO**

FAMILY IS A SUPERPOWER

CAPSTONE EDITIONS

a Capstone imprint

Throughout the universe, a single superpower outshines all others.

An ever-changing, ever-growing power found within the World's Greatest Super Heroes . . .

. . . and everyday heroes, like you.

With this superpower, a hero is never alone . . .

. . . and always has a place for one more.

. . . and strength in every difference.

With this power,
a hero need not
be afraid . . .

. . . *because it overcomes every fear.*

Within each hero, this superpower grows stronger every day . . .

With this superpower,
a hero always has a
helping hand . . .

This superpower keeps a hero afloat . . .

. . . and rescues them from the deepest depths.

This power is a hero's
constant companion . . .

. . . even as time flashes by.

For no matter where a hero is going . . .

. . . or where they began . . .

. . . one superpower is always within.

The power of **family.**

FAMILY POWER CHECKLIST!

☐
Support

☐
Strength

☐
Encouragement

☐
Belonging

☐
Commitment

☐
Love